Jane Yolen

Welcome to the
RIVER OF GRASS

Illustrated by Laura Regan

G. P. Putnam's Sons · New York

With special thanks to Professor Don Kroodsma
of the University of Massachusetts for bird advice,
and Rick and Jean Seavey, Everglades National Park,
Homestead, Florida.

Text copyright © 2001 by Jane Yolen.
Illustrations copyright © 2001 by Laura Regan.
All rights reserved. This book, or parts thereof, may
not be reproduced in any form without permission
in writing from the publisher, G. P. Putnam's Sons,
a division of Penguin Putnam Books for Young Readers,
345 Hudson Street, New York, NY 10014.
G. P. Putnam's Sons, Reg. U.S. Pat. & Tm. Off.
Published simultaneously in Canada.
Printed in Hong Kong by South China Printing Co. (1988) Ltd.
Designed by Gina DiMassi. Text set in Meridien Medium.
The art was done in gouache on illustration board.
Library of Congress Cataloging-in-Publication Data
Yolen, Jane. Welcome to the river of grass / Jane Yolen ;
illustrated by Laura Regan. p. cm. 1. Wetland ecology—
Florida—Everglades—Juvenile literature. [1. Everglades (Fla.)
2. Wetland ecology. 3. Ecology.] I. Regan, Laura, ill. II. Title.
QH105.F6 Y65 2001 577.68'4'0975939—dc21   00-038230
ISBN 0-399-23221-4
10 9 8 7 6 5 4 3 2 1
First Impression

To Refna Wilkin, welcome indeed
—J. Y.

For Jane and Refna, with admiration
and gratitude
—L. R.

"... the Indians, who have known the Glades
longer and better than any dictionary-making
white man, gave them their perfect and poetic
name: 'Pa-hay-okee' ... 'Grassy Water.'"

—Marjory Stoneman Douglas

Welcome to the river of grass,
running green
from side to side,
a river that is inches deep
and miles wide.

Tree islands hump up
over the grass,
clump up
into hummocky hammocks
covered with vines:
live oak,
myrsine,
pigeon plum—
making green clouds
of trees crowding
the horizon.
Islands of cabbage palm,
willows,
formed on top of
rotting peat pillows.

Early morning:
A white-tailed deer—
a doe and fawn—
walk through the saw grass
silent as the sun,
eat quickly,
then move on.

A brief shudder in the water,
proclaims an otter.
And a tuft-eared bobcat on the prowl;
makes itself known
with an eerie *yoooooowl*.

Farther south
by the mangroves
on stiltlike roots
the water goes brackish,
then brine.
A raccoon hunts around,
then dines
on tasty shoots,
on crabs or oysters,
washing his food
to make it moister.
Then off to bed,
to sleep out the day.

EXTENSION

Above, on a mangrove snag,
an osprey,
with dagger beak and nail,
guts a fish
from head to tail.

Full day:
Overhead
a great blue heron
flies,
while mostly under fresh water
lies
a hungry alligator in wait,
its shroudlike eyes
implacable as fate,
till a redbelly turtle,
a singular swimmer,
comes too close—
and is alligator dinner.

All unnoticed,
above his head
darning needles, damsel flies
on iridescent wings,
live their brief lives.

Up from the water,
an anhinga lands
on a limestone rock ledge
or a fallen tree limb
by the water's edge
spreading its wings,
to catch the sun.
Then when this drying task
is done,
once again it flies off to seek
its fishy meal
with spear-sharp beak.

Palmetto bugs,
like shiny brown leaves,
weave in and out of the grass.
They pass
spiderwebs spun out across
resurrection ferns
that the first soft rains
have startled into life.

Life and death
come quick
to the brown applesnail
not far from its eggs
on the pickerel weed leaf.
Far above sails
the freewheeling kite
alert for the snail
which it breaks with its beak.
Meanwhile a company of butterflies,
Heliconius,
named for the sun,
is left alone
to flutter by.

Twilight:
The sky's deep blue slate
is written on
by passing birds:
the calligraphy
of ibis,
egret,
spoonbill,
stork,
at twilight returning
to roost in the dark.

And a barred owl,
silent winging,
dark-sighted,
a low, hooted singing,
waits as well—but for the night—
when at last he will take flight,
his great wings fanned and steady,
his eyes and ears ready
to take his living from the land.

A single panther,
rare and rarely seen,
brown against the fading green,
gazes into the coming night
all prepared for instant flight
across the saw grass,
the river,
the hammocks,
the park,
and well into advancing dark.

A shadow, he fades away at last,
welcome as we are,
to this river of grass.

Did You Know?

The Everglades ecosystem, in places over fifty miles wide but averaging only a few inches deep, once began with the lovely meandering Kissimmee River flowing into Lake Okeechobee and spilling southward over its banks into the broad Everglades wetlands. It was a place of marvel and enchantment, best known for its most popular denizen, the alligator. It also had the richest assortment of plants, animals, fish, snakes, amphibians and insects found in the continental United States.

But humans have changed the Everglades significantly, beginning in the early part of the twentieth century when great canals were excavated throughout South and Central Florida. Then dikes were built, and dams, so that the waters could be carefully controlled. Why? To drain large sections of land for farming and development as well as providing the east coast of Florida with a more dependable source of fresh water.

With this drainage, vast colonies of wading birds vanished—a ninety percent reduction in fifty years. Feral pigs imported for hunting crowded out indigenous species. Even the mighty Florida panther, once a popular denizen of the area, all but disappeared.

Even though the Everglades was declared a National Park in 1947, these endangerments continue. By 1996 the Everglades was cited as among the most threatened rivers of North America.

Today, with the urging of such groups as the Everglades Coalition and Friends of the Everglades, there has been a struggle to reverse the misfortunes of the Everglades. But ecosystems are very delicately balanced.

Sometimes what is lost can never be regained.

To learn more about the Florida Everglades, contact:

Florida Everglades
Visitor Center
(305) 242-7700

There are several good websites:

www.everglades.national-park.com
www.florida-everglades.com
www.everglades.org